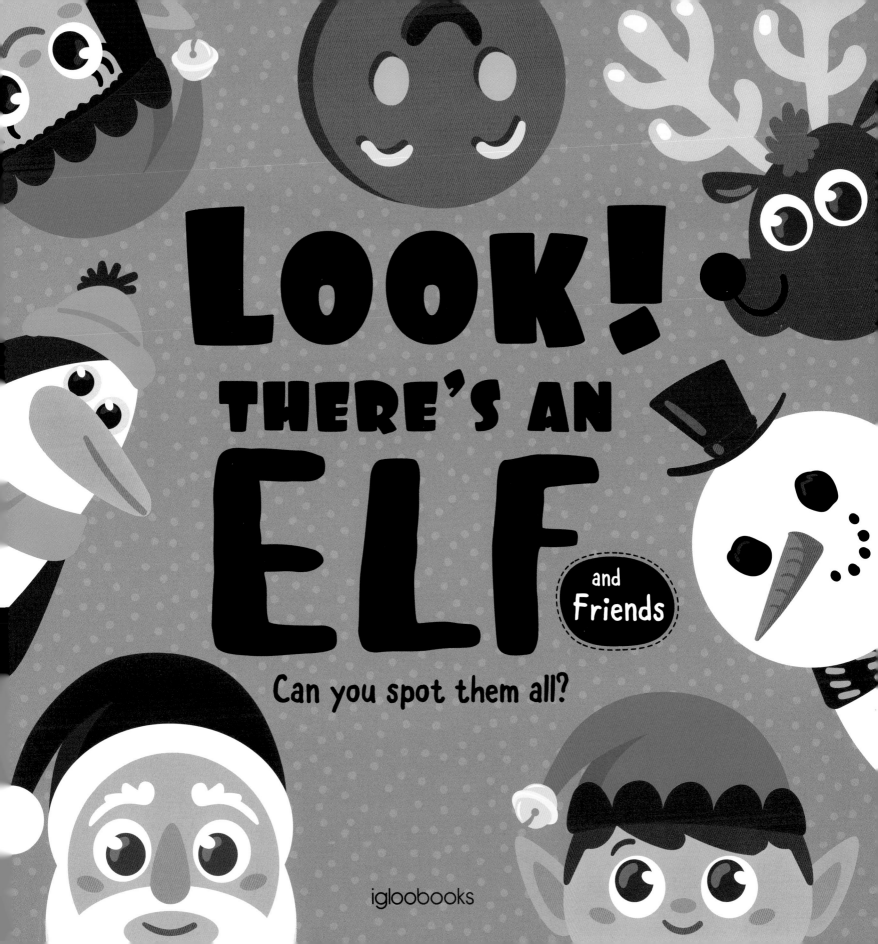

LOOK! THERE'S AN ELF.

and Friends

Can you spot them all?

igloobooks

MEET THE CHRISTMAS CREW!

Time for some festive fun! Ten Christmas characters are hiding on every page in this fun book. Read the profiles below to learn all about their personalities, then look carefully at the scenes to find where each one is hiding. Answers are at the back of the book so you can check your seasonal searching skills!

SANTA

HOBBY:
Writing lists

MOST EATEN SNACK:
Mince pies

SECRET SKILL:
Climbing

JULIET

FAVOURITE COLOUR:
Green

HOBBY:
Taking s-elfies

FAVOURITE RESTAURANTS:
S-elf service

JOHN

KNOWN FOR:
Elf-confidence

FAVOURITE MUSIC:
Hip hop and wrap

SECRET SKILL:
S-elf taught
bell ringing

MARY

FAVOURITE SONG:
Jingle Bells

FAVOURITE BOOK:
The Night Before
Christmas

KNOWN FOR:
Festive spirit

MARIAH

KNOWN FOR:
Swimming skills

MOST-USED PHRASE:
Have a n-ice day!

FAVOURITE HOLIDAY DESTINATION:
Anywhere n-ice

ARTHUR

FAVOURITE TREAT:
Ice pops

KNOWN FOR:
Being a cool guy

MOST-USED PHRASE:
I'm chilling

GWEN

MOST EATEN SNACK:
Rainbow cake

FAVOURITE WEATHER:
Rain

MOST-USED PHRASE:
Oh, deer!

KEVIN

KNOWN AS:
A high-flier

FAVOURITE SONG:
Let It Snow!

FAVOURITE SAYING:
Hoof a great day!

GEORGE

FAVOURITE STORY:
Goldilocks and the Three Bears

KNOWN FOR:
Cuddly bear hugs

FAVOURITE ACCESSORY:
Christmas jumper

SUSAN

KNOWN AS:
A snappy dresser

LOVES:
Anything sweet

MOST-USED PHRASE:
Oh, crumbs!

TREE-MENDOUS TOWN

It's beginning to look a lot like Christmas in this
snowy town! Where are all the festive friends hiding?

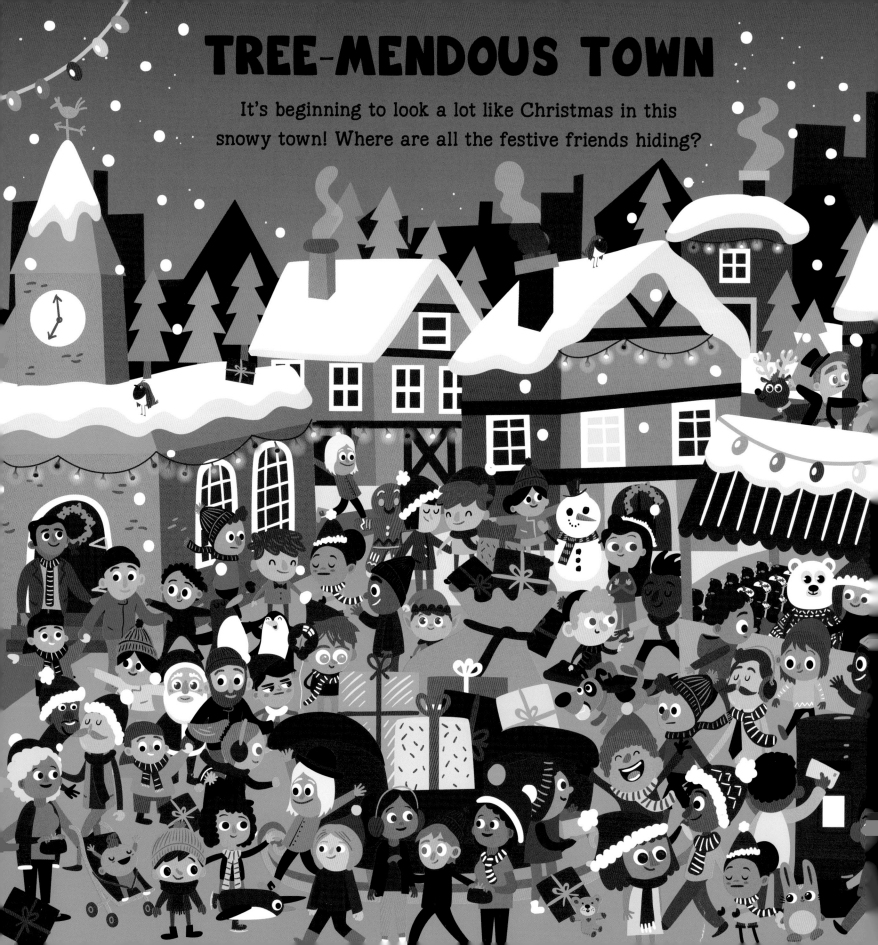

CAN YOU SPOT THE GREEN CANDY CANE?

MAGICAL TOY SHOP

Santa and his friends are in the toy shop checking that all the children are being good. Can you spot all ten festive pals?

CAN YOU SPOT THE LITTLE BLUE DUCK?

MERRY COAST-MAS

Search this seaside scene for Santa and his friends
enjoying the sunshine. Look carefully, they're hidden well!

CAN YOU SPOT
THE WREATH?

FESTIVE FUNFAIR

When they are not busy preparing for Christmas, the festive friends love fairground rides. Can you spot them all?

THAT'S A WRAP

The presents are being wrapped and loaded on the sleigh.
Try to find all ten characters in this busy scene.

CAN YOU SPOT THE CAMERA?

SUN, SEA AND SANTA!

It's time for a break and some fun in the sun.
Can you spot the friends in this busy beach scene?

CAN YOU SPOT THE JAR OF SWEETS?

FESTIVE FARM

Even the animals on the farm like to celebrate Christmas.
See if you can spot each festive friend in the farmyard.

CAN YOU SPOT THE RED HAT?

CHRISTMAS ON ICE

The skates are on and everyone is slipping and sliding on the ice.
The friends are great skaters, but where are they?

CAN YOU SPOT
THE RED MUG?

SWEET TREATS

Look at all the yummy sweets! The festive friends are
hiding here somewhere. Can you find them all?

CAN YOU SPOT THE RED STOCKING?

SAFARI SLEIGH RIDE

Uh, oh! It looks like Santa's sleigh has taken a wrong turn and landed in the jungle! Look closely to find all of the festive gang.

CAN YOU SPOT THE SNOW GLOBE?

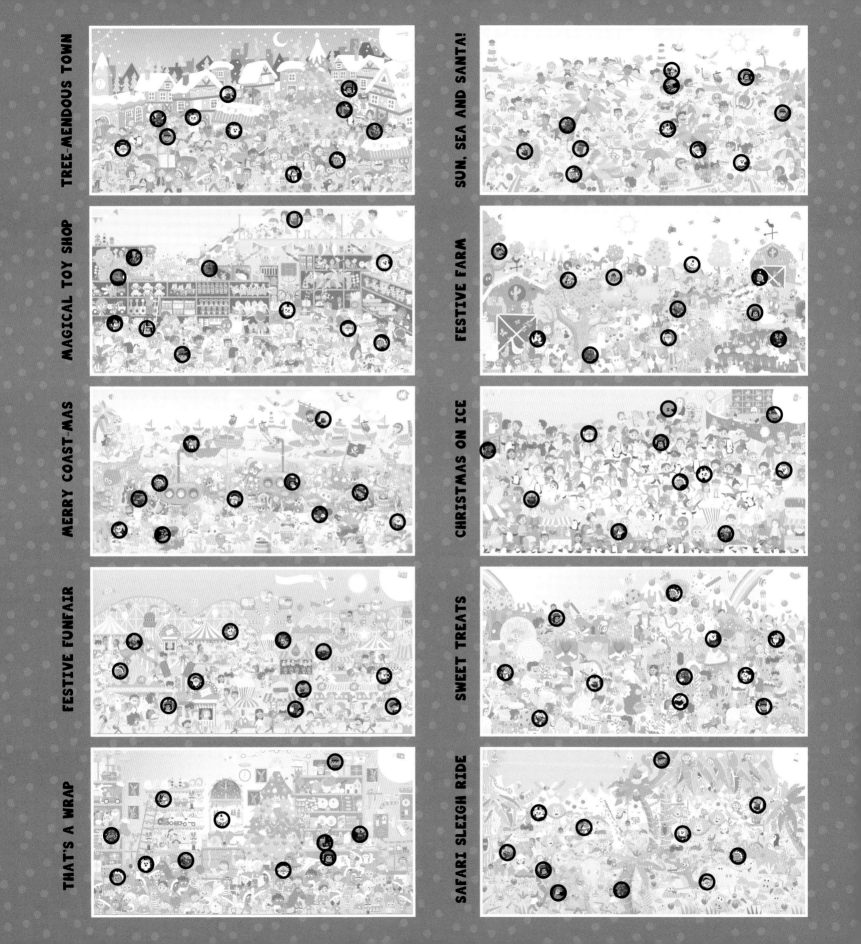

TREE-MENDOUS TOWN

SUN, SEA AND SANTA!

MAGICAL TOY SHOP

FESTIVE FARM

MERRY COAST-MAS

CHRISTMAS ON ICE

FESTIVE FUNFAIR

SWEET TREATS

THAT'S A WRAP

SAFARI SLEIGH RIDE